Amazing Dragonflies

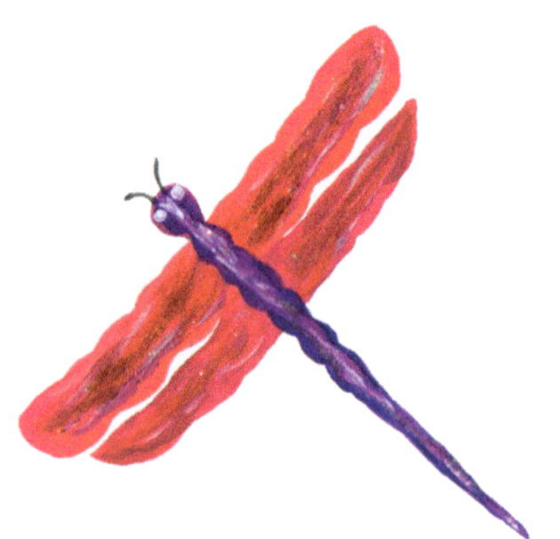

Amazing Dragonflies

Fairy Tales from Distant Stars
Matarika Stories

Written, illustrated and designed
by Malgorzata Polczynska

edited by Arya Shoup

To All Animals

On the planet Matarika, life was peaceful and pleasant, and everything worked in harmony.

The inhabitants often met at the Gathering House to share new inventions, ideas, and creations. Children and adults enjoyed singing, dancing, sharing stories, and playing together.

There were also moments of silence in which everyone directed feelings of deep gratitude toward the planet, suns, moons, and all the creatures that dwelled here. These moments strengthened everyone's understanding of each other, allowing them to better communicate and work toward mutual growth.

The meetings were especially liked by children, who also spent time learning about their own character and personality traits and how to develop them in the best possible way.

Maika and Valey often helped organize the children by leading activities and caring for the younger ones. Because the twins were the only survivors of their generation and had more experience connecting with nature, they were highly respected by the other children.

However, Maika and Valey were different from the other children in another important way. They carried the memories of all the children who had died during the planet's catastrophe. They didn't feel it as a burden but more as something strengthening and supportive.

On each anniversary of the explosion, the twins meditated near the place where the golden threads of their brothers' and sisters' lives had been broken. There was a stone placed there, engraved with an image of a beautiful four-petaled Gaura flower. Maika and Valey connected with the incredible network of golden threads that they still had in their hearts. Although the other children had not survived, the twins knew that somewhere in the far reaches of space, their energies still existed and could connect with them, and they felt as if those children were still somehow alive in them.

Maika and Valey worked to be joyful every day so as to pass on the most beautiful energy to these children.

One day, while Maika was helping Lamana gather and sort herbs, Valey ran over to them, panting heavily.

"Quickly, quickly!" cried Valey. "A dragonfly was crushed by a big rock. I found it struggling in one of the old crevices. We have to help save her wing!"

Lamana turned to Maika. "Maika, dear, I'll go with Valey, and you can go get the Great Mothers."

The Shaman and a group of other nearby inhabitants were soon on the scene of the accident. A few adults managed to lift the heavy stone and carefully pull out from under it the delicate wing of the dragonfly. The wing was torn and bruised.

Lamana said, "Before the Great Mothers came, we used to treat injuries like these with special herbal ointments, but the treatment took a very long time, and the dragonflies could not fly for many days. Maybe this time the Great Mothers could help to cure this wounded wing more quickly?"

The Great Mothers arrived with Maika and began to examine the wing and check the health of Lady Dragonfly. They put her in a comfortable position and asked everyone to surround her in a wide circle, holding hands, because such shared, heartfelt energy greatly accelerates healing. Then, all three Great Mothers, gently holding the huge wing, started to connect its torn parts with golden threads that appeared under their hands. It all looked magical, and everyone could feel how the common energy of the planet, suns, and moons, as well as the inhabitants, supported this healing process.

Maika and Valey perched close and observed everything the Great Mothers did.

After the procedure was completed, Lady Dragonfly was transported to the Dragonfly Waterfall. It was a favorite resting spot for all insects, and there, too, other dragonflies could help and keep her company.

Lamana and the twins agreed to look after the insect. The whole family of dragonflies was extremely grateful to the residents for the quick help in saving their injured friend.

The twins spent a good deal of time with their wounded patient. Every day, they brought Hibi herb leaves and fresh water from the waterfall, and they picked tiny sweet Oli fruits for her to eat, which were the favorite treat of all dragonflies. Both children were truly pleased that they could be so close to the dragonfly because such an opportunity was extremely rare. Maika and Valey were curious about how dragonflies live, and they had many questions for her.

After a few days of care, the dragonfly appeared to feel much better, and Valey thought that she opened her eyes and smiled slightly at him.

So he asked if she needed anything else, and if she would like to talk for a moment, or tell them something about herself.

"We know that dragonflies have been on Matarika for a very, very long time, even before the first inhabitants appeared," the boy said.

"But where did you come from and when did you arrive? And what was our planet like then?" he continued.

The dragonfly smiled wide and stretched her uninjured wing.

Maika hugged her tenderly. "We love you very much. We love watching dragonflies soar in the sky, and we know that you are helping us a lot," she whispered in the dragonfly's ear. "If you would like to tell us something about yourself, we would be very happy. We don't hear words from you, but we can read energy, and it comes into our minds as if it were words."

"First of all," answered Lady Dragonfly, "I'd like to say that I am grateful for your help. I was so tired from the long flight from the other side of the planet, and I wanted to rest for a moment by the rock, and then the stones began to fall from above, and I couldn't fly away in time. But Valey found me quickly."

"Yes, I heard a strange sound and ran in that direction, and I noticed you under those rocks," said the boy. "And I told you not to be nervous because I'll get help right away."

"It was lucky for me that you did," confessed the dragonfly. "Everything turned out well, and now I'll be all right. My wing is recovering, and my energy is coming back. So, I'd love to tell you the story of dragonflies, but it is quite long."

"That's all right," replied Valey. "We are very interested in your story, aren't we, Maika?" And they both made themselves comfortable near the patient's head.

"Well, then," started the dragonfly. "I was born on Matarika, but my ancestors came from a very distant planet that was created long ago, almost at the beginning of all Creation, a place called the Luminous Dragonfly Planet. There live dragonflies of various colors and sizes. Some of them are tiny, and some are huge, but all of them have four transparent, shiny wings that connect at their hearts. Our wings are extra sensitive, and they collect information from the surrounding environment. The information travels to our hearts and is shared with other dragonflies and finally runs to the heart of the Spirit of the Animal Kingdom, so that our Spirit knows what is happening in the places where the dragonflies live.

"From the Luminous Dragonfly Planet, many of the dragonflies migrate to different places in the universe. There was once a planet inhabited by many different families of insects. There were wasps, flies, beetles, ladybugs, fireflies, and grasshoppers. Many dragonflies chose to migrate there.

"However, this planet was ruled by big wasps. While all the other insects agreed the wasps were clever, they didn't like how the wasps argued among themselves a lot as each of the three big wasp families wanted to be the most important.

"They competed fiercely with each other until two families together enslaved a third family and banished its queen to the desert. The queen would surely have perished for lack of water had it not been for the dragonflies that carried her to a remote, shaded place where there was a small well and a little rain. On the way, the dragonflies took turns feeding and watering her, and they discovered that the queen was carrying dozens of small eggs of future young wasps. The journey was long and tough, but luckily, the queen's babies were born after she had arrived in this safe place. This new family of wasps was grateful for all the help, and the tiny, young wasps walked on the wings of dragonflies, buzzing happily, thinking they were their relatives." The dragonfly smiled reflectively.

"This is how a friendship was established between dragonflies and wasps, as well as other insects that were glad to live nearby. Over time, the wasps created comfortable new habitats in this safe place, which they happily shared with other insects."

"And what happened to those other two families of wasps?" Valey wanted to know.

"Well," Lady Dragonfly continued, "those two families were still competing with each other, and there came a great drought that decimated both families. Most of the enslaved wasps also died out.

"Word reached them that somewhere in the far south of the planet, other big wasps lived in abundance and safety. So, some of the wasps from those two families wandered the long and dangerous way, hoping to find support and help there. A few of the enslaved wasps were also taken to serve others, but along the way, any differences between all the wasps ceased to matter.

"And here I must say that dragonflies also helped these wasps during their migration. When the new and old wasp families met, they had a long talk with each other, and the old wasps were allowed to settle near the habitats of the new wasp families. But new rules were established so that they all would support and help each other. It was an amazing lesson for all wasps, and the dragonflies played a supportive part."

"But how did you come here to Matarika?" asked Maika curiously.

"Oh, yes, that is next in the story," the dragonfly carried on. "On the planet of wasps, the dragonflies lived well and had their own comfortable place among the high rocks and ponds. But one day, a meteorite hit the planet, and part of the rock where the dragonflies lived was chipped off and thrown into space.

"It was as if the Spirit of the Animal Kingdom had decided that some of us should move to a new place.

"So, it came to be that my ancestors huddled in a crevice of a rock and came to Matarika. After arriving, the dragonflies found a big waterfall, where there were stones for dragonfly eggs to develop safely. Soon, however, the dragonflies noticed that the planet had a problem. In some places, a poison that looked like yellow snowflakes flowed up into the air from the interior of the planet. When these flakes settled onto the planet's surface, they destroyed plants and infected small insects that already lived on the Matarika.

"There were also colorful long-haired cows on the planet," the dragonfly continued, after taking a few sips of water from a Hibi herb leaf. "But these flakes did not harm them because the cows had lived here since ancient times, and they themselves cleaned the surface of the planet from various substances that were unhealthy for other beings."

Lady Dragonfly took a deep breath, and after a while, she said, "And now, I will tell you the most important thing of all.

"The dragonflies proved to be resistant to the poisonous effects of the yellow flakes. My ancestors began to purify Matarika's atmosphere by catching these flakes on their vast wings and rinsing them with water from the waterfall. The poison flowed back into the planet's interior, where it was purified by many layers of soil.

"Over the years, dragonflies have managed to clean Matarika's air completely because they were diligent and brave."

"How is it possible that other insects were dying, but dragonflies were resistant and even able to help?" Valey asked.

"My ancestors asked the same question," responded the wounded dragonfly. "Do you remember how I told you that baby wasps loved to walk on dragonfly wings? You see, the wasps have poisonous stingers, so when these little wasps sat on the wings of dragonflies, they made them immune to the poison of their stings. So, even without knowing it, dragonflies had become more and more resistant to poisons and so were able to help so many other beings."

"Dragonflies are amazing!" exclaimed Valey.

Lady Dragonfly smiled. "Thank you. Sometimes we ourselves are amazed at how beautifully it all works together. The Spirit of the Plant Kingdom and the Spirit of the Animal Kingdom exchange information with each other, and then everything balances out."

Maika and Valey cuddled up to the dragonfly, wanting to express their gratitude for what dragonflies have done for the entire planet.

Lady Dragonfly seemed to be getting worn out by this long talk as her eyelids drooped, and she started yawning.

"We'll leave you to rest now," whispered Valey. "We've brought you more water on Hibi herb leaves and also those little Oli fruits you like so much."

"Tomorrow we'll come again and bring the Great Mothers to check on your wing. Thank you so much, Lady Dragonfly," added Maika.

The children wanted to share with Lamana what they had learned of the dragonfly's long history. They were also curious what the shaman had remembered from the past days, as she was the oldest inhabitant of the planet. So they spent the evening with her by a small fire, sharing their thoughts and feelings.

The next day, the Great Mothers, Lamana, and a large group of residents visited the dragonfly. The wounded wing was healing quickly, and the Great Mothers washed it with clean spring water and left the dragonfly to rest.

After a few more days, Lady Dragonfly felt much better and even tried to fly a little. Soon, she was completely healed and ready to soar in the skies with the other dragonflies once again.

The inhabitants have always respected the serenity and space of the dragonflies, and when Maika and Valey told them the amazing story they heard from Lady Dragonfly, their admiration and gratitude toward these creatures increased even more.

One day, while Maika and Valey were visiting the memorial stone for the children who died in the catastrophe, they realized something new. The engraved image of the four-petalled Gaura flower looked very much like the wings of a dragonfly. The children soon mentioned this to Lamana, and she explained that, after the explosion, the dragonflies collected the remnants of the golden threads on their wings and deposited them in the place where the monument now stands.

"Our children have flown off into far space, but the memory of them is honored within the heart of the four petals, just like the dragonfly connects its wings to its heart," explained the shaman.

"It's such a beautiful symbol," Valey said reverently.

Since discovering this, whenever the twins visited the memorial, they remembered the story of dragonflies and their amazing winged feats.

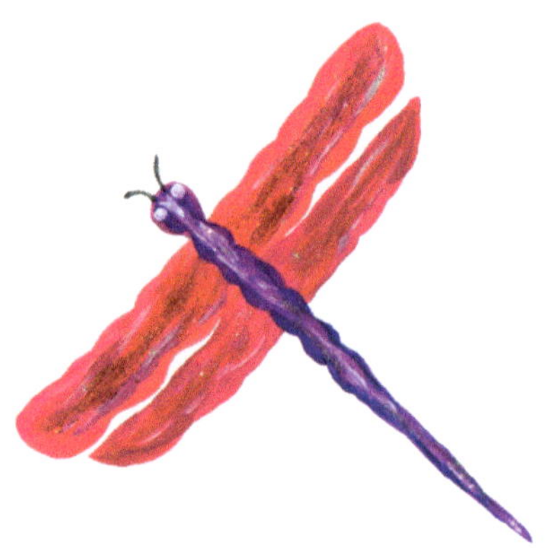

Coming soon in the series
"Fairy Tales from Distant Stars"

Matarika Stories
5 / Noble Cows

Already published
1 / The Girl Who Saved the Planet
2 / Great Mother
3 / A Tree Full of Wonders